ESCAPE FROM
THE NETHER

ESCAPE FROM THE NETHER

AN UNOFFICIAL MINECRAFTERS TIME TRAVEL ADVENTURE

BOOK FOUR

Winter Morgan

Sky Pony Press
New York

Copyright © 2019 by Hollan Publishing, Inc.

Minecraft® is a registered trademark of Notch Development AB.

The Minecraft game is copyright © Mojang AB.

Sky Pony Press books may be purchased in bulk at special discounts for sales promotion, corporate gifts, fund-raising, or educational purposes. Special editions can also be created to specifications. For details, contact the Special Sales Department, Sky Pony Press, 307 West 36th Street, 11th Floor, New York, NY 10018 or info@skyhorsepublishing.com.

Sky Pony® is a registered trademark of Skyhorse Publishing, Inc.®, a Delaware corporation.

Minecraft® is a registered trademark of Notch Development AB. The Minecraft game is copyright © Mojang AB.

Visit our website at www.skyponypress.com.

10 9 8 7 6 5 4 3 2 1

Library of Congress Cataloging-in-Publication Data is available on file.

Cover design by Brian Peterson
Cover art by Bill Greenhead

Print ISBN: 978-1-5107-4117-1
Ebook ISBN: 978-1-5107-4130-0

Printed in Canada

TABLE OF CONTENTS

ESCAPE FROM THE NETHER

1

RUNNING ON EMPTY

Brett stood over his crafting table and stared at the empty bottles. "It seems like we have a lot of bottles but nothing to fill them with," he remarked as he picked up a bottle and looked inside.

"We're out of Nether wart, ghast tears, and blaze rods," said Poppy.

Their friends Helen and Nancy walked inside Brett's house. "Are you guys planning another prank?" asked Nancy.

Poppy laughed. "I wish. We have no time to plan pranks. We're out of potions. There isn't an alchemist in the town, so we can't buy any. We need to get a bunch of supplies from the Nether, or we'll never be able to make more potions."

"Look at how many bottles we can fill." Brett pointed to the rows of empty bottles that lined his crafting table.

Nancy and Helen looked through their inventories. As Helen surveyed her potions, she told them, "I'm very low on potions, or I'd lend you some."

"Same here," said Nancy. "It's been awhile since we traveled to the Nether. Perhaps we should go on a trip."

Poppy grimaced. She disliked the Nether. Although she had been there multiple times and learned several tricks to survive, she didn't enjoy visiting the hot and inhospitable biome. "Do I really have to go to the Nether with you guys? Can't I just stay here, and you can bring back Nether wart and the other stuff we need, and I can trade with you guys?"

Brett was surprised. "Poppy, nobody likes to travel to the Nether, but we all do it because we have to gather ingredients for our potions. You can't stay behind."

"Seriously? But I'll trade with you," Poppy pleaded.

Helen agreed with Brett. "You know Brett is correct. This isn't something anybody wants to do. If we all go together, we'll work as a team and get everything we need to craft potions. We won't be there too long."

"Yes," added Nancy. "It will be a quick trip. We don't have to search for treasure unless you guys want to. Do you?" Nancy loved treasure hunting and would find any opportunity to unearth diamonds and other valuables that were found in a Nether fortress.

"I am definitely not going to search for treasure. You're lucky I'm even going to the Nether," proclaimed Poppy.

Brett didn't like the way Poppy was acting, and he asked Poppy if she would walk outside with him. As they stood underneath an apple tree, Brett picked an apple and handed it to Poppy.

"Thanks. Why did you give me an apple?" she asked and then took a bite. "I didn't ask for one."

"I gave you the apple because I'm your friend and I saw that your health bar was low. Friends do nice things for one another, and they are thoughtful."

"Thanks," said Poppy.

"You're welcome. But do you know why I asked you to come outside?"

Poppy didn't reply.

Brett said, "I just wanted you to know that I don't care for the way you're acting."

Poppy felt a lump in her throat. She knew Brett was right, she wasn't being nice about the trip to the Nether, but she had an excuse: she disliked the Nether. However, she had to admit that she didn't personally know anyone who enjoyed a trip to the Nether. She pulled obsidian from her inventory. "I'm sorry. I'll craft the portal."

"Great." Brett smiled. "Tell the others."

While Poppy went into the house to tell Helen and Nancy that she was crafting a portal, a familiar voice called out in the distance.

"Brett!"

Brett looked up and saw Joe racing toward him, his blue hair waving in the wind. "Joe!" Brett exclaimed. "It's been awhile. What are you doing in Meadow Mews?"

"I was asked to create a farm in Verdant Valley, and I was hoping you'd be able to help me. It's just a small project, but with your help, we could probably finish it in a few days."

"I'd love to work on the farm, but I was about to go to the Nether with Poppy, Helen, and Nancy."

"Can you do that in a few days?" asked Joe.

"No, we are about to craft the portal. We have no potions left in our inventories," explained Brett.

Joe looked through his inventory. "I'm also running low on potions. Perhaps I can do a quick trip to the Nether with you guys. I don't start the project for a few days."

"Wow, that's perfect. I'd love to work on the farm with you after we get back from the Nether."

"Amazing. This is great timing," said Joe.

The duo raced inside the house. Brett was excited Joe was back, and he was anxious to announce that Joe would be joining them on the trip to the Nether. But they were so excited, he didn't have a chance to tell them. The gang cheered the minute they saw Joe walk through the entrance to Brett's house.

"Joe!" Poppy called out. "I feel like we haven't seen you in forever." She held the obsidian in her hand and pointed toward it. "We are going to the Nether right now. Want to come?"

"He's joining us," answered Brett.

"I'm so excited to gather ingredients with you guys," said Joe.

"Great," Poppy said. She walked out of the house and announced, "Let's all create the portal."

As Poppy placed the first piece of obsidian on the

ground, a loud thunderous boom rattled Meadow Mews. Rain began to flood the ground, saturating the lone piece of obsidian. The gang raced toward Brett's house, but a barrage of arrows flew at them.

"Ouch!" Joe called out as an arrow ripped through his black leather jacket and pierced his shoulder.

Brett quickly pulled his diamond armor from his inventory and put it on, then grabbed his diamond sword and raced toward the skeletons advancing in their direction. Brett slammed his sword into the bony beasts, destroying them. The rest of the gang suited up in armor, except Joe, who was still wailing in pain.

"Joe, are you okay?" asked Brett.

"I will be fine." He looked in his inventory for a potion to regain his strength, but there wasn't anything there. He pulled out a glass of milk and took a quick drink, then put on his diamond armor and readied himself for an attack against the skeletons. Luckily he had his armor on when another arrow struck him. This time he didn't feel any pain, as the arrow grazed his diamond armor. He sprinted toward the skeleton and ripped into the rattling bones with his diamond sword. As Joe swung his sword, the rain stopped, and the remaining skeletons disappeared.

"What an annoying rain shower," remarked Helen.

Poppy looked down at the obsidian on the ground. "This isn't damaged. We can still craft a portal."

The gang put down obsidian, and they ignited the portal. They hopped on, and a purple mist surrounded them.

2

NETHER EXPECTED THIS

There wasn't even a moment to warn one another about the sudden attack. The purple mist was still clouding their vision when Nancy screamed out in pain, "My leg burns!" She lost a heart. Three ghasts flew above them, shooting a succession of fireballs at the gang.

"Ouch!" Brett cried out as a fireball singed his leg. Poppy handed him a bottle of milk and instructed him to drink it to increase his health bar. Brett sipped the milk and grabbed his bow and arrow. He tried to shoot at the ghasts, but another fireball landed on his arm, and he dropped the bow and arrow. As he reached for the bow and arrow, he was struck by another fireball. Despite drinking the milk, he had only one heart left. He was fading, and his energy was almost depleted.

"Help!" he cried out as another fireball flew toward him.

Poppy pushed Brett out of the way, and the fireball landed on her armored chest. She shot an arrow at the ghast and destroyed it. A ghast tear fell to the ground, and she quickly picked it up and placed it in her inventory. She pulled out another bottle of milk and handed it to Brett. "You will be okay." She smiled.

Brett didn't have time to thank Poppy. The second after he ingested the last drops of milk, he shot an arrow at a ghast and destroyed it. Nancy, Helen, and Joe aimed their bows and arrows at the final ghast, then destroyed the flying menace. Ghast tears dropped down, and the gang was soon happily refilling their inventories.

Joe looked up. "It looks like we won't have to battle any flying mobs for a while. The sky is clear."

Nancy called out, "Look guys! I see a Nether fortress."

Poppy squinted. "Where? I don't see one."

Nancy pointed. "It's far off in the distance."

The others stood by Nancy and looked at where she was pointing. Brett said, "I don't see it, but let's travel in that direction. You might have better vision than we do."

"It's there, I promise," said Nancy.

"I hope you're right," said Joe as he walked behind Nancy.

"You don't believe me." Nancy was annoyed.

"We do," Brett explained, "but we just don't see it."

"You're a treasure hunter," Helen told Nancy, "which means you have better instincts and can spot Nether fortresses."

Helen stopped to look at the lava waterfall, which

was flowing into a long lake that lined the path to the Nether fortress. Nancy said, "Don't stop. We have to keep going."

"I hate to admit this," said Helen, "but there is something very beautiful about lava."

"I don't think lava is beautiful," grumbled Poppy.

Poppy wanted to leave the Nether as fast as she could. She didn't like being there, and everyone knew it. She hoped Nancy was correct and that they were headed in the right direction. It seemed as if they were following her for a long time, and they still hadn't reached the Nether fortress. She wondered if Nancy was wrong. Maybe she didn't have great vision. Poppy questioned, "Nancy, are you sure you saw the Nether fortress? I feel like we have been walking forever."

"I promise you, the Nether fortress is not much farther. Just follow me," Nancy replied.

Poppy hoped Nancy was correct. Sweat formed on Poppy's forehead, and she was very thirsty. She stopped to take a drink from her inventory.

"Why are you stopping?" asked Nancy.

"It's so hot. I just despise the Nether," she said as she sipped her milk.

"Nobody likes the Nether," said Joe.

Helen called out, "I see it!"

"You do?" asked Poppy.

"Yes, Nancy is right," said Helen. "Look ahead. There's a Nether fortress."

Poppy stared ahead and saw the Nether fortress.

She was relieved and apologized to Nancy. "I'm sorry I'm complaining. Thank you for finding the fortress."

As they made their way to the Nether fortress, four zombie pigmen walked past them, and Poppy tried not to lock eyes with them. She didn't want to battle anyone. She just wanted to get to the Nether fortress and get the Nether wart and other supplies.

The Nether fortress was in view, and the gang picked up their speed. Before they could race toward the entrance, Nancy called out, "Stop!"

The gang halted. Nancy pointed to a small cavern-like structure that was surrounded by mushrooms and dead shrubs. Poppy asked, "What's that?"

"It's a cavern. They are very rare. We have to go inside," Nancy said as she walked toward the cavern's entrance.

"Why? We are so close to the Nether fortress. Why do we have to take a detour?" Poppy questioned.

Joe replied, "Nether quartz. Am I right, Nancy?"

"You are correct," said Nancy. "This is the only place we can get it. Let's mine in this cavern and then head over to the fortress."

Poppy didn't fight back. She just followed her friends into the cavern. She knew Nether quartz was a rare find and very valuable. She pulled out her pick-axe and joined them for the quick trip to unearth the quartz. However, the trip wasn't quick, and the gang mined for a while before one of them found the precious quartz. When they finally found a bunch and were satisfied with the amount they unearthed, they exited the cavern, but as they left, they were surrounded by another group of ghasts.

"Not again!" Brett called out as he put his pick-axe away and pulled out his bow and arrow. The gang evaded the harsh burns from the fireballs while they shot arrows at the red-eyed beasts. The creatures unleashed a loud, high-pitched scream when they were hit by the arrows.

A fireball burned Joe's shoulder, and he wailed and lost a heart. He had one heart left, and Brett wanted to hand him a glass of milk to help him recover, but he didn't have a chance. More ghasts flew toward them and shot more fireballs. One hit Brett, and he also cried out in pain. Another fireball struck Joe, and he vanished.

"Joe!" Brett cried as a second fireball hit him, leaving him with only one heart. He shot arrows at the ghasts, but they didn't seem to have any impact on this hostile Nether mob. They weren't being destroyed, and the group wasn't being rewarded with ghast tears. Another fireball hit Brett, and he awoke in his bed in the middle of a rainstorm.

The rain fell down on his roof, and he could hear the sounds of skeleton bones rattling outside his window.

"Brett!" A faint familiar voice called in the distance. "Help!"

3
IN THE RAIN

Brett jumped out of bed and raced toward the window when he heard the voice call out again, "Brett! Help!"

It sounded like Poppy, but he thought she was still in the Nether with the others. Brett readjusted his armor and took a large gulp of milk, then rushed out of his bedroom. When he entered his living room, he saw his front door being ripped from its hinges.

Brett clutched his diamond sword as he watched two zombies rip his door off. He held his breath to avoid puking from the rancid odor of rotting flesh. Brett slammed his diamond sword into the zombies' stomachs, destroying the undead beasts. When they were gone, he gasped for air and sprinted outside into the rain.

Skeletons crowded around the streets of Meadow Mews, and the residents were outside battling the bony beasts. Brett joined his neighbors in battle as he kept a close eye out for Poppy. He hadn't heard her cries in a while, and he was wondering if he had imagined it. Brett swung his diamond sword at a skeleton that lunged at him. The sword cracked one of the skeleton's bones, which infuriated the bony beast. The skeleton retaliated by shooting two arrows at Brett, which cost him two hearts. Brett slammed his diamond sword into the skeleton again and destroyed it. While sipping some milk to aid in his recovery, he heard another voice call out to him.

"Brett!" Joe said, "I'm here!" and raced toward Brett.

"Have you seen Poppy?" asked Brett.

"No, I thought she was in the Nether," said Joe.

"I did too, but I thought I heard her call out to me, and I can't seem to find her. This worries me," Brett said as he leaped at a skeleton that stood inches from him.

"What is up with this zombie and skeleton invasion?" asked Joe. "I mean, we have rainstorms, but they never produce this many hostile mobs."

"Do you think something more sinister is happening?" Brett questioned as he slammed his sword into a skeleton.

"I hope not. I just want this to end so we can go to Verdant Valley and create the farm," said Joe as he destroyed a fetid-smelling zombie with his diamond sword.

Brett also wanted this to end and was looking forward to spending a few days with his friend in Verdant Valley, but that seemed so far off. It seemed as if they were never even going to make it back to the Nether. The rain fell harder, and the streets of Meadow Mews were saturated in water. Puddles formed all around them, and their feet were soaked. The rain fell into their eyes, clouding their vision, and Brett was exhausted.

An army of skeletons marched through the village, and Brett and Joe gasped. Despite having some help from the residents of Meadow Mews, they were going to have an intense battle. They were outnumbered. Brett told himself that he would do as much as he could to stop the skeletons, but he knew this might be a losing battle.

Brett raced toward the army with his diamond sword in his hand, and Joe sprinted beside him. As they ripped into the first few skeleton soldiers, they heard a voice.

"Help me! Brett! Help me!"

"It's Poppy!" Brett cried, but Joe didn't hear him. Joe was too immersed in the battle against the bony beasts.

Brett rushed toward the voice, and Joe called out, "What are you doing? Are you abandoning me?"

"No, come with me! I hear Poppy, and she needs our help!"

Joe couldn't hear Brett's words because thunder boomed and lightning struck a nearby tree. The tree tumbled, and Joe narrowly avoided being struck by the tree. He had no idea where Brett was going, and he felt as if one of his best friends had betrayed him. Joe called out, "Brett! Come back!"

Brett could hear Joe's scream for him to come back,

but he wasn't going to turn around—he had to find Poppy. He heard her call out again.

"Brett! Help!" she cried and then wailed in pain.

"Where are you, Poppy?" hollered Brett, but there was no response. He jogged toward the direction where he had heard her voice and slipped in a puddle, landing on the ground. He looked up and saw Joe.

"What is wrong with you? Why would you abandon me? We were battling skeletons," Joe complained. "And the skeletons are following us here."

Arrows shot through the sky, and Brett tried to avoid them as he steadied himself and got up from the damp muddy ground. When he finally stood up, they could hear Poppy call out.

"Please come quick! I need help!"

Brett didn't have time to respond to Joe, but Joe knew why Brett had left. They had to find Poppy and help her. Thunder boomed through the town as lightning struck again. Joe called out, "Poppy, we are trying to find you!"

"I'm over here!" she cried out, but they couldn't see her.

"Where?" Brett shouted. "We can't find you."

"Help! Quick!" Poppy cried out again.

Brett's heart raced. He wanted to help his friend, but the rain, the skeletons, and the lightning were slowing him down. Brett felt a stinging pain radiate down his arm. He knew he was struck by an arrow, and turned around to destroy the skeleton. As he looked back, he saw over a hundred skeletons clustered together. They all held out their bows and arrows and shot at Brett and Joe, destroying them instantly.

Brett awoke in his bed and was shocked to see the sun was out. He sprinted from the house and looked for Poppy and Joe. He called out their names, but he didn't get a response. The only voice he heard was Nancy's.

"What happened to you?" Nancy asked as she spotted Brett racing around Meadow Mews.

"Is anybody still in the Nether? I am looking for Poppy."

"Poppy is with Helen," said Nancy. "We were all destroyed in the Nether, and then we were destroyed again by the skeletons and zombies."

"I was with Joe, and we were also destroyed by the skeletons," said Brett.

Joe hollered in the distance, "Brett, Nancy. I'm back."

Nancy said, "We have to go back to the Nether, and we have to do it right now. Something strange happened when we were down there."

"What?" asked Joe as he caught his breath and stood next to them.

"We made it into the Nether fortress, and we heard something," she explained.

Poppy and Helen raced over to them. Poppy blurted out, "Did Nancy tell you what happened?"

"Not yet," said Brett. "She was just telling us."

Nancy finished, "Someone is trapped in the Nether fortress, and we have to free them."

"We must go back to the Nether," said Poppy eagerly, "and we have to do it now." She pulled obsidian from her inventory and started to craft a portal.

4

BEHIND THE WALL

Brett had never seen Poppy this eager to go to the Nether. She spoke rapidly as she built the portal. "When we were in the Nether fortress, we could hear someone crying from the other side of a wall, but before we could find out who they were, we were attacked by wither skeletons."

"I heard you calling out for help last night," said Brett.

"Yes, I was about to be destroyed by skeletons. I knew you were back in Meadow Mews, and I was calling for help," she said as she placed another piece of obsidian on the damp ground. Despite the sun, the grass was still wet from the rainstorm.

"I felt bad. We tried to find you, but we couldn't," said Brett.

Joe added, "It was an intense battle. We didn't even survive."

Nancy and Helen shook their heads. Nancy said, "I

19

don't get why these hostile mobs have to spawn in the rainstorm. There are so many of them, too. It seems like with each storm, the attacks are getting worse."

Everyone agreed, and they theorized if this would continue and what they could do about it, but they didn't come up with any concrete ideas. The conversation stopped when Poppy placed the final piece of obsidian on the ground. She called out, "Hop on!"

The gang stood together on the portal while Poppy ignited it. Purple mist enveloped them, and they landed in the Nether. This time ghasts didn't greet them, and the skies were calm as they walked along the lava river toward the Nether fortress.

They didn't see any hostile mobs until they reached the fortress, which was guarded by a group of blazes. The blazes rose from the ground as they approached and began to attack. Brett remembered he had a bunch of snowballs in his inventory and handed them to his friends.

"These are great for annihilating blazes," he said as he threw the snowball at the hostile mob. It struck the blaze and destroyed it. The freezing, wet snow had felt nice in his warm hand. He didn't like the severe heat in the Nether. He pulled another snowball from his inventory and placed it against his forehead, immediately cooling him down, and then threw it at a blaze. Blaze rods and glowstone dust fell to the ground as the final blaze was destroyed. The group gathered the dropped items up quickly as they raced inside the Nether fortress.

"Don't we have to pick up the Nether wart?" Brett questioned as they raced past the staircase, which had a large section of Nether wart. They hadn't emptied the fortress for supplies.

"We will get to that, but we have to help this person," said Poppy as she made her way through the dimly lit fortress toward the room where they heard the person call for help. Poppy put her hand against the wall. "Do you hear us? We're back and we can help."

There was silence.

"Where is the person?" asked Joe.

"They were on the other side of the wall when we were here," said Poppy.

"Are we sure this is the right fortress?" questioned Joe.

"It should be." Poppy called out to the person again, and when she didn't hear a response, she also started to question if they were in the wrong fortress. "Maybe you're right, Joe. Perhaps this isn't the right fortress. There are many fortresses in the Nether, and we might have spawned in another section of it."

"We should empty this fortress. We need a lot of ingredients for our potions," Brett said as he exited the room and walked toward the stairs. He needed to pick up the Nether wart. He didn't want this trip to be a waste. They still were lacking a lot of materials for potions, and he didn't want to be attacked again and then have to make another return trip to the Nether. He pulled the Nether wart and the soul sand from the edge of the stairs, and the others joined him.

Joe stopped picking Nether wart when he heard a

strange noise nearby. "Do you hear that?" he asked the others.

Boing! Boing! Boing! Boing! The noise came from the other room. Brett knew that sound and said, "That sounds like magma cubes." He pulled his diamond sword from his inventory. Brett was correct. Within seconds, the bouncing, menacing cubes were in the middle of the room.

Brett and Joe sliced into a large cube, which broke into smaller cubes. The gang used all of their strength as they slammed their swords into the mobs' red-and-black skin and annihilated the blocky mob. When the final magma cube was destroyed, the gang let out a collective sigh of relief. However, they didn't have a long time to relax, because within seconds they were under attack again.

Two wither skeletons leaped at the gang, hitting Nancy with their swords. As the gang fought the wither skeletons, they could hear a muffled voice call out.

"Help me!"

Brett slammed his diamond sword into the belly of the wither skeleton, destroying the beast with one whack. The wither skeleton dropped coal. Joe destroyed the other wither skeleton, which dropped a bone. They picked up the drops and bolted toward Poppy. She was racing in the direction to where she heard the voice.

Poppy called out to the voice, "We can hear you. Are you okay?"

"Help!" the voice called out again.

"Are you okay?" Nancy yelled at the top of her lungs.

Again, they were met with silence.

"What's going on?" asked Poppy. "Why can't they hear us?"

"We want to help you," Brett hollered. "Tell us who you are."

"Help!" the voice called out again.

"I don't think they can hear us," said Helen.

Brett took out his pickaxe and slammed it against the wall of the Nether fortress, making a small hole in the wall. He tried to see through to the other side, but it was too dark.

"Can you see anything?" asked Poppy.

"Can you give me a torch?" asked Brett.

She handed Brett a torch. He held it close to the small hole, but he still couldn't see what was on the other side. He slammed his pickaxe against the wall again, and this time the hole grew larger. He raised the torch toward the hole and looked in.

"I don't think there is anything on the other side. It just looks empty," said Brett.

Poppy pushed Brett out of the way and screamed into the hole, "We are here to help you. Are you okay?"

There was silence, and then after a minute, they could hear someone faintly reply, "No."

5

RESCUE MISSION

Brett slammed his pickaxe against the wall, and the hole grew. The rest of the gang pulled pickaxes from their inventories and ripped into the wall until it crumbled to the ground. They hopped over the rubble and searched for the person who was on the other side, but the room looked empty.

"Are you there?" asked Poppy.

"Yes," the voice called out.

"Where?" Poppy questioned as she looked around the room.

"Here," they replied, but the voice was even weaker than before.

"It sounds like they are over here," said Joe as he spotted a door.

"Open it," said Poppy.

As Joe opened the door, the group was caught in a whirlwind of frigid air. Brett's teeth began to chatter and he realized he had felt this feeling before. "Oh no!" Brett cried. "We are entering a portal."

Joe had already walked through the door, and Poppy was following him. Brett looked back at Helen and Nancy. "This isn't good. We are going to wind up in another time period in the Minecraft Universe." His voice shook as he spoke and his teeth clattered together.

"We can't abandon our friends," said Nancy as she pushed Brett forward through the door and into the cold unknown.

Brett was freezing. He called out to Joe and Poppy, but there was no response. Unlike the other trips through time portals, this one didn't force him to fall down a large hole. With this portal, he simply walked through a doorway and into a large hallway that was as cold as a freezer. He wished he had a jacket, because his blue T-shirt wasn't doing the job. Brett called out to his friends again, but he didn't hear a response. He took a deep breath and made his way down the long cold hallway. At the end of the hallway was a wooden door. It was ajar, and Brett walked inside the room.

"Brett." Poppy smiled. She was standing next to a person with long green hair and a red jacket. She was handing them a bottle of milk.

Brett was happy to be reunited with his friends. He was also happy that the room was warm. However, he knew they weren't in the same period. He just had to find out if they were in the future or the past. He said, "We just walked through a portal. I have no idea if we are in the past or the future, but we aren't in the present."

"Are you sure?" asked Joe.

"Certain of it. I've been through a few portals, and they were all eerily cold like the hallway we just walked down," said Brett.

"I'm not concerned with the time period," said Poppy. "I just want to help this person."

The woman with green hair gulped the milk. After her health bar was replenished, she spoke. "Thank you," she said.

"Where are we?" asked Brett.

"I don't know," replied the woman. "I mean, I know we're in the Nether, but I don't know where we are in relation to where you came from." She paused. "I hope I don't sound too confusing. I'd like to introduce myself. My name is Eva. I've been stuck in this room for a long time."

"Why?" asked Nancy.

"Somebody trapped me here. I'm afraid that when they find out that I'm gone, they will come looking for me again," said Eva.

"Who trapped you here?" questioned Helen.

"Theo the Alchemist. He terrorizes the Overworld. I used to be a very respected alchemist, but he trapped all of the alchemists from around the Overworld because he didn't want anybody competing with him."

"That's awful," remarked Nancy.

"I know. Once I get out of here, I am going to look for all of my alchemist friends. We were on a group trip to the Nether to gather supplies when he found us. He was able to isolate all of us and trap us. He has a big army," explained Eva.

"How long have you been in here? When did this happen? Do you think he will come back?" Helen spat a ton of questions at Eva.

"Um, I don't know," she said nervously. "I can't actually answer any of those questions. I feel like I have been here forever, but since there is no day or night in the Nether, I can't figure it out at all."

"That makes sense," said Poppy. "But it really doesn't matter how long you've been down here. We have to get you out of here."

Everyone agreed they had to build a portal back to the Overworld. As they sprinted through the Nether fortress, Brett wondered what time period the portal would drop them in. He looked back at the door. He wanted to suggest that they travel through it back to their time period, where Eva would be safe. However, he knew they had to return Eva to the time period where she belonged. As they made their way through the fortress, Joe cried out in pain.

A wither skeleton slammed its sword into Joe's back as they were exiting the fortress, leaving Joe with one heart. Nancy gave him milk to replenish his health, and Brett slammed his diamond sword against the wither skeleton, but it wasn't an easy battle. Brett leaped toward the wither skeleton and swung at it, and he was surprised at his own skill. He had destroyed the wither skeleton and quickly picked up the bone it had dropped on the floor, then followed his friends out of the fortress.

The landscape didn't look anything like the one

they had seen earlier that day. There were three lava waterfalls and multiple zombie pigmen walking around the Nether. There was a large bridge built of netherrack, and two people dressed in yellow stood on it, looking out at the fortress.

"Who are you?" the people shouted.

"Oh no!" cried Eva. "Those are Theo's soldiers. He makes them dress all in yellow."

"What should we do?" asked Nancy.

Eva said, "Theo took all my weapons and everything from my inventory. If I had a bow and arrow, I'd use it."

Nancy and Helen took out their bows and arrows and aimed at the two people dressed in yellow. Nancy and Helen unleashed a barrage of arrows. The two people called out for them to stop and asked for help, but it was too late. Nancy and Helen destroyed them.

Poppy built the portal, and they all hopped on it. As they were surrounded in purple mist, Brett wondered if they should trust Eva. How did they know she was telling the truth? Maybe she was the bad guy and was being watched by the people in yellow? Why did they believe everything she said? The purple mist grew heavier, but Brett could still make out Eva's face through the purple-colored mist. He saw her smirk. He was curious to know if she was smiling because she was happy she was free or if she smirked because she had just captured her newest victims.

6

DESERT RAIN

Brett's heart raced as they stood on the portal. Although the journey back to the Overworld took seconds, it felt like an eternity. Brett couldn't stop staring at Eva. He wanted to keep a close eye on her because he didn't trust her. He had to watch her actions and find out if she was telling the truth. Eva noticed Brett watching her, and she turned to look at him.

"Is everything okay?" she asked.

"Yes, there is just purple mist in my eyes," he said, rubbing his eyes and then looking down at his feet.

Once the mist faded, Brett noticed the endless sandy terrain and the extreme heat. He was hoping to get a break from the heat and cool down, but he was out of luck because they were in the middle of the desert.

"Is this where you live?" asked Poppy.

"No," Eva replied. "My town is gone. Theo destroyed it." Her eyes filled with tears.

"That's awful. I'm sorry to hear that," Joe said.

"Where did you live?" asked Nancy.

"It was a small town called Farmer's Bay," said Eva.

"Farmer's Bay!" Joe called out. "That's where I live."

"I don't recognize you," said Eva.

"That's because this is a different time period," said Brett. "We have to go back to Meadow Mews and find out what time period this is. We can ask our future or past selves."

"You can't go back to Meadow Mews," said Eva.

"Why not?" questioned Brett.

"Theo destroyed Meadow Mews ages ago," Eva explained. "I never even went there. I've only read about it in history books."

"What? Meadow Mews is gone?" Poppy cried.

"Let's go back to where it used to be and see if there is anything left," suggested Nancy.

"Before you go back to find a demolished town, can you help save the people left in the Overworld? I know Theo is set on destroying it all. Once he finds out that I've escaped, he will come looking for me, and I'm afraid it will be dangerous for all of us," said Eva as she wiped tears from her eyes and sniffled.

"I think we should look for Theo. Stop him before he comes after you," suggested Brett.

"I agree," said Poppy. "We don't want to wait around to see if we are attacked or waste all of our energy hiding from him."

As Poppy spoke, thunder boomed through the town and a heavy rain fell on the desert, making the sand thicker and harder to walk on. "What?" exclaimed Joe. "It never rains in the desert."

"It rains every day in the Overworld. At least ten times a day," said Eva. "What are you talking about?"

"It wasn't always like that," said Brett.

"I never knew a time when I didn't have to battle mobs in the rain," said Eva. "And now my inventory is empty, and I can't even battle. I am doomed."

Brett handed her a diamond sword from his inventory. She thanked him as she grabbed the sword and lunged at a skeleton that spawned inches from her.

Brett didn't even have to turn around to know there was a zombie behind him; he could smell it a mile away. He swiftly turned around and struck the zombie, plunging his sword into the zombie's rotten flesh. Once he obliterated the zombie, he raced toward a skeleton that was ready to destroy Eva and slammed his sword into its bony frame. He picked up the bone it dropped on the ground when it was destroyed, and he handed it to Eva.

"Thanks." She smiled.

"How long do these rainstorms last?" he asked as he struck another skeleton that stood behind Eva.

Eva leaped at a zombie, destroyed it, and took a deep breath before she replied, "There is no time frame. Some last hours, some minutes."

This rainstorm was lasting longer than a minute, and the group was getting tired. They were still low on potions and only had a few bottles of milk to help them recover. They tried not to sustain any injuries from the attacks, but it was impossible. Helen and Nancy were both down to two hearts, and they only had one bottle of milk between them. Everyone was on edge, which was why they all shuddered when they heard the loud clanging of bones and saw a massive skeleton army marching toward them.

"What are we going to do?" asked Poppy.

"I wish I had potions," said Eva. "The only item I have is Brett's diamond sword. Do you guys have any potions I can borrow?"

"We don't have any potions. That was why we were in the Nether," Poppy explained, but there wasn't time to discuss their lack of potions because within seconds they were face-to-face with a large skeleton army. Arrows flew through the sky, and they tried to duck.

"Help!" Eva screamed.

When Brett slammed his sword into the first skeleton, the sun came up, and the army disappeared.

Eva said, "We have to be prepared. There could be another attack at any time. It's funny, but when I was imprisoned in the Nether, I made myself feel better by reminding myself that at least I didn't have to deal with these daily attacks in the rain."

"I can't believe you live in a world that is under constant attack. We experienced a bit of it before we left on our trip to the Nether, and it was awful," remarked Poppy.

Brett said, "What if the attacks that we were

experiencing in Meadow Mews were just the beginning of a larger attack? Perhaps Theo was just starting to destroy Meadow Mews?"

"I'm not sure Theo is behind the storms, but that does make sense. I just know that he has an army and they take over property and force people to change their skins and join the army. He also won't let anyone else practice alchemy," said Eva.

"We have to find out if he is behind the storms. He could be controlling them with command blocks," said Brett.

"I wonder where he lives," said Joe.

"I've never seen where he lives," said Eva. "People say that it's in the cold taiga and he houses all of the people in a large ice castle. They even say he has a farm, which I find very hard to believe. How can you make a farm in the snow?"

"We've done it," said Joe, "and I bet Theo is hiding in the cold biome that we worked on."

"And I'm sure he's housing his soldiers in the ice castle I created with my friends Callie and Laura," said Poppy.

"Do you guys remember how to get to the cold taiga?" asked Eva.

"When we worked there, it was called Hillsdale," said Brett.

"Hillsdale." Eva paused. "It doesn't sound familiar to me."

Joe said, "I think we can find it, but we need to be prepared before we leave for the journey."

"How?" asked Eva. "I don't have a home, and I have an empty inventory. How can I prepare to attack Theo and his army?"

Poppy said, "We have to get out of the desert and find an area where we can pick fruit and vegetables and hunt. Also, I am a builder. I can make a house for us, and we can set up a crafting table and brew potions. We have to take a break and plan. It's the only way we can save you and our town."

"I know there is a pasture right outside the desert. If you'd like, we can stay there and try to create a farm and make a house," said Eva.

"Can you lead us there?" asked Poppy.

"Of course," Eva said.

Brett was glad they were going to spend a few days with Eva. He wanted to study her. He was beginning to trust her, and he hoped that she wasn't setting them up to be trapped.

7
FAMILIAR FINDS

Brett kept waiting for the rain, but it never came. He was relieved when they finally reached the pasture and saw the remnants of a farm. "Joe, we can work on this farm while the others build the house," he said.

Poppy led the group to a shady stretch of land and began to construct the house. Eva kept apologizing because her inventory was empty and she couldn't offer any wooden planks or other items one needed for building a house.

Brett and Joe inspected the ground. There was an irrigation system in place, and wheat still grew in some patches. Brett pulled a potato from the ground. "It looks like they had a nice farm here. I wonder when it was destroyed," said Brett.

"It's so sad to think that this is the future. I'm so glad we are here and have a chance to help everyone and change the future of the Overworld. I'd hate to know that Farmer's Bay and Verdant Valley didn't exist. I can't live in a world like that."

Brett nodded. He didn't want to live in a world that was under constant threat from a bully named Theo. He looked over at his friends and marveled at how quickly they constructed the house. Poppy was putting in a window. He loved the way she worked so well under pressure. They had been through a lot together, but she still amazed him.

"Looks like we have a place to head to if it starts to rain." Brett pointed to the house.

"Wow," exclaimed Joe. "They did a great job. That's such a nice house."

It *was* a nice house. It was larger than they expected, and there was a long picture window that looked out at the farm they were building. Brett saw them place a door in the frame and walk inside the house. He hoped they were crafting potions.

Joe placed seeds on the ground. "We should have crops in a few days. We still need more food. Perhaps we should hunt."

Brett wasn't very good at hunting, but he knew they had to get a few chickens for dinner. "It seems like there aren't many animals around here. Have you seen any?"

"No," said Brett. "That's weird. I wonder if Theo has done something with the animals."

A loud voice called out, "Did somebody say my name?"

A man wearing a yellow robe appeared and stomped on their freshly planted row of seeds.

"What are you doing?" asked Joe. "We just planted those."

"You can not create a farm without my permission," Theo screamed, "so I must destroy it."

"Who made up that rule?" Brett asked as he pulled his diamond sword from his inventory.

"I'd put that away if I were you," warned Theo.

"Why?" Brett asked as he pointed the sword at Theo.

"You know, I've never seen you guys before," said Theo, "so you must be new and must not understand how the Overworld works. If you put down the sword, I'll teach you."

"I am not putting down the sword. Why don't you explain it to me anyway?" asked Brett as he moved the sword closer to Theo's chest.

"Army!" Theo called out, and within seconds a group of people dressed in yellow surrounded Brett and Joe.

"Army commander," Theo called out. One of the soldiers came forward, and Theo instructed him, "Take these men to the jail."

"No," Brett said, but he knew fighting was pointless. He followed the soldiers through the pasture and into the cold taiga.

Brett and Joe instantly recognized the taiga. Joe said, "This is Hillsdale."

"You're right." Brett stared at Poppy's well-designed ice castle and recalled when she built it with her two friends. He looked over at the farm he had created with

Joe. He saw soldiers dressed in yellow picking various foods. He began to salivate when he saw the lush farm filled with potatoes and apples. He wanted to race over and scream, "This is our farm, and we deserve this food," but he didn't say anything. He just walked in the direction of a bedrock prison that was constructed next to a snowy mountain.

Joe reached down on the ground and made a snowball. He placed it in his inventory. One of the soldiers noticed and asked him what he was doing. "I was just keeping it in case I go to the Nether."

The soldier laughed. "You're not going anywhere."

"Can I keep it?" asked Joe.

"You can't have anything in your inventory. Once we put you in jail, we empty it all. So you can keep it until we enter the prison. Enjoy it for the next minute." The soldier chuckled.

Brett wanted to plan an escape, but he didn't know what to do. He also had a few snowballs in his inventory, and he thought about throwing them at the soldiers, but it would be a waste. The soldiers outnumbered them. As they walked toward the bedrock prison, they heard a loud noise.

"A storm!" one of the soldiers screamed.

"Be prepared," another solider called out.

This time the storm brought a gusty wind and snow. Skeletons spawned, and they appeared camouflaged in the white snowy landscape. Arrows flew at the soldiers. Brett and Joe tried to shield themselves from the arrows by standing behind the soldiers.

"Run!" Brett screamed to Joe.

Dressed in armor, the two sprinted out of the cold taiga and toward the pasture, avoiding attacks from hostile mobs as the snow turned to rain. After a while, it stopped. It was almost night when they finally reached the pasture. A lone skeleton walked in the dusk and aimed its bow and arrow at the guys.

Brett lunged at the skeleton, annihilating it with one hard strike. He picked up the dropped bone and said, "We have to warn the others."

Joe hurried toward the house; Brett walked behind him. By the time Brett reached the front door, he saw Joe standing outside of the house. He was pacing and talking to himself.

"Joe, are you okay?" asked Brett.

"I don't understand what happened," Joe said, and he repeated this statement as he paced back and forth in front of the entryway.

"Let me go in. I want to see Poppy," Brett demanded.

"No," said Joe.

"Why not?"

"I don't understand what happened," said Joe.

"What do you mean?"

"Look inside." Joe's voice cracked as he spoke. "The h-house," he stuttered. "It's empty."

8

HOT AND COLD

Brett walked inside the house, and it was eerily empty. There weren't any beds or signs that anybody had been there. He walked through the entire house, but he didn't find anything. Joe was still pacing in front of the house. He called to him, "Joe, come in."

Joe reluctantly walked inside. "What did Theo do to them? Where are they? Where are the beds? I thought they had enough time to make beds and even craft potions. Where is it all? And where are our friends?"

"We will find them," said Brett calmly.

"Will we?" asked Joe. "We might not. And we might be trapped in this time period forever. We were almost prisoners in a bedrock prison with no possibility of escape. How can you be so calm?"

"I don't see the point in *not* being calm. We have to come up with a plan. We know we have to save our friends, save the Overworld, and especially save Meadow Mews from being destroyed."

"That's a lot," Joe said and then added, "I don't think we can win our battle here."

"What?" asked Brett.

"We have to go back in time to save the future. This part of the world is done. We can't destroy Theo in the future; we need to destroy him in the past, before he could cause all this damage."

"But how? We don't have a time machine," said Brett. "We never get to choose when we go back and forth in time. It always seems so accidental."

"We will have to figure out how to either make a portal or find a portal," said Joe. "It's our only hope."

"Do you think we should travel back to the Nether?" asked Brett.

"We can," Joe said. He looked out the window. It was dark out, and he saw two block-carrying Endermen off in the distance. "But we should stay here for the night. It's too dangerous for us to go out. We could be attacked."

"Don't you think it's dangerous for us to stay here? I think the soldiers will come looking for us," said Brett.

"It might be, but we don't have a choice."

"I guess you're right," said Brett.

"Do you have the supplies to craft a portal to the Nether? I think we should go back there in the morning and see if we can go back in time through the Nether fortress," suggested Joe.

Brett started to think about heading to the Nether, and it made him feel uneasy. He didn't feel right heading back into the past without Poppy, Nancy, and Helen. He could never forgive himself if they were stuck in the future forever. He had no idea where they were, but he had to find them. He expressed this to Joe: "I don't think we should leave without our friends."

"I agree, but where are they? Do you think they are in the bedrock prison?"

Brett didn't think they were there. "If they were placed in the prison, we would have seen them. I wonder if they saw what was happening to us and hid. Maybe they are in the cold taiga now trying to save us," theorized Brett.

Joe said, "That actually sounds like a real possibility, but how are we going to go back to the cold taiga without getting caught?"

"We will have to be very careful. Hopefully we can find them as we travel there," said Brett.

"Do you think it will work?"

"I don't know," Brett said as he crafted a bed, "but I think we should sleep here tonight and get up the minute the sun comes up and look for them."

Joe was weary and worried that they would be caught in the middle of the night and brought back to the prison, but he felt he had no other choice than to craft a bed and go to sleep.

As they crawled into their beds, there was a sound at the door.

"What's that?" asked Brett.

There was no time to respond. A zombie ripped the door from its hinges and attacked them with its extended arms. Brett plunged his diamond sword into the zombie's smelly flesh.

"There are more!" Joe pointed to two more zombies lumbering through the doorway. He raced toward them and held his breath as he struck the undead beasts with his diamond sword.

When the final zombie was annihilated, Joe and Brett placed the door back in the doorway.

"I'm exhausted," said Joe as he yawned.

"Me too, but I hope we can sleep. I'm worried Theo will come soon," said Brett.

"I feel the same way, but we agreed we have to stay here," said Joe.

"I know." Brett crawled into the bed, pulled the wool blanket over himself, and then said, "Good night."

That night they both slept lightly, worrying that they would be caught. Brett tossed and turned until he finally fell asleep. When he awoke in the morning, he looked over at Joe's bed. It was empty.

9

MOMENT IN THE MINE

"Joe?" Brett called out, but there was no response. Brett sprinted outside and was shocked when he saw Poppy talking to Joe by the farm.

"Poppy!" Brett called out as he raced toward his friend. "You're here!"

Poppy spoke quickly. "We have to get out of here. The others are hiding in a mine outside of town."

Brett and Joe followed Poppy to the mine. They raced through the pasture and toward a hilly biome, where she led them down a path shaded with trees.

"How did you find this place?" asked Brett.

"Eva," she replied breathlessly. She pulled out a torch and entered the small musty cave.

"Brett! Joe!" the others called out. "Poppy found you."

Nancy said, "I didn't think she would. We were so worried. She told us we should stay back here and she knew she'd find you guys."

47

Eva was standing by a brewing stand. "Do you guys want any potions? I am brewing potions for everybody. So far we all have a potion of invisibility."

Eva walked over to Brett and Joe and handed them bottles of potion. "These are yours."

Brett told the group how they were taken to a prison in the cold taiga. "It was Hillsdale, the town that we worked on, Poppy. They do house everyone in your ice castle."

Joe added, "They eat the food from our farm. I was devastated."

"At least we know that area very well," said Poppy. "That will help us. I know the layout of the ice castle, and I also did something that I do with all of my homes. I put in a secret room."

"You put a secret room in all of your designs? I didn't know that." Brett was shocked. He thought he knew everything about Poppy and now he discovered that she had placed secret rooms in all of the buildings she designed in the Overworld.

"Yes," confessed Poppy, "and I have one in the ice castle. If we can get in there, maybe we can put TNT blocks in that room and blow up the ice castle."

"And destroy the beautiful creation," said Brett.

Joe interrupted with, "I don't think we should bother fighting Theo now. I mentioned to Brett that we have to go back into the past to save the future. We have to attack Theo at an earlier stage."

"How can we do that?" asked Eva.

"We need to go back to the past through the portal in the Nether," said Joe.

"Let's do it," Eva said, "but first let me finish brewing these potions."

"Do we have time?" asked Joe.

Brett stood next to Joe and saw a pair of red eyes in the corner by Joe's feet. He quickly grabbed his sword and swung it at the spider. Joe jumped out of the way. "You could have warned me. You scared me."

"Sorry," said Brett. "I saw a spider."

"Great, I can use a spider eye," said Eva as she worked on a potion. Brett handed the spider eye to Eva, and she completed a potion. "I want to give everyone some potions for harming and healing, and then I think we can get to the Nether. I am excited to travel back in time and see Meadow Mews. I've only heard and read about it."

The gang collected the potions and placed them in their inventories. They bolted out of the mine and were about to craft a portal when they heard the thunder.

"We have to do this fast," said Poppy.

"It's too late," cried Nancy. "We don't have enough time."

Skeletons and zombies spawned and surrounded them. They didn't want to waste their potions on this battle, and they fought tirelessly using their diamond swords, bows and arrows, and energy. Brett slammed his sword into a zombie that seemed to have never-ending strength. No matter how many times he slammed his sword into its gross-smelling flesh, it still leaped at him.

Joe slammed his sword into the zombie that attacked Brett and destroyed it. Bones rattled as the gang fought the group of zombies that shot arrows at them. The rain was falling hard, and the ground was becoming muddy. The group tried not to slip as they battled the beasts in the rain.

Poppy wasn't waiting for the storm to end. She gathered the supplies to craft a portal to the Nether and placed them on the wet ground. She wanted to be ready to ignite the portal the second the rain stopped. As her friends battled the mobs, she carefully placed all the pieces of obsidian on the mud, and when the final raindrop fell and the last skeleton and zombie disappeared, she called out, "Hop on!"

The gang clustered together as they traveled back to the Nether. The purple mist faded, and they were in the middle of the Nether, but there wasn't a Nether fortress in sight.

"Where's the Nether fortress?" asked Eva.

"I don't know, but we'll find it," said Poppy.

Brett hoped Poppy was correct. They set out to search for a Nether fortress, and they all hoped it wouldn't take a long time. Every second spent in the Nether was always dangerous, and this trip was no exception. A group of ghasts spotted them and unleashed a collective high-pitched shriek as they slammed the group with fireballs.

As they shot arrows at the ghasts, Brett heard

somebody call out, "You think you can escape from me?"

He turned around to see Theo and his army.

10

THE PORTAL

Brett didn't know where to aim his bow and arrow. Ghasts flew overhead spitting out a succession of fireballs as Theo and his army shot arrows at the gang. Brett's leg was burned, and an arrow struck his shoulder. He had one heart, and he tried to grab the potion of healing Eva had brewed for him, but he was destroyed before he could take a sip. The potion spilled onto the netherrack ground, and Brett awoke in the house Poppy had built in the pasture. He wasn't alone.

"Get up," a soldier screamed at him.

"Okay," said Brett. "Please don't yell."

"We won't yell if you get up right now and follow us to the prison," said the soldier without raising his voice.

Brett stood up, and the soldier asked him to empty his inventory. Brett's heart began to race. He didn't want to empty it. If he did, he wouldn't have any way to defend himself against an attack. He pulled one bottle of milk from his inventory and fumbled with it. He handed it to the soldier.

The soldier prodded Brett with the sword, and Brett cried out in pain. The soldier said, "You're going to have to move a little faster."

"I'm sorry, but I am moving as fast I can." Brett's voice cracked. "Giving up everything in your inventory isn't an easy thing to do. It took me a long time to acquire all of these items."

The soldier didn't care if Brett thought this was hard and slammed his sword into Brett's unarmored shoulder. "Faster! Empty the inventory!"

As Brett handed over every item from his inventory, he heard a noise outside the large picture window. One of the soldiers looked out the window and ordered the other soldier to go outside and destroy anyone he saw there. The soldier raced from the house and immediately called out for help, but before the other soldier could help him, he was destroyed by Poppy.

Poppy raced into the house with Nancy. Nancy leaped at the soldier with her diamond sword, striking him until he was obliterated.

"Brett," said Nancy, "we have to go back to the Nether. I think we can get into the portal."

"Where are Joe, Helen, and Eva?" asked Brett.

"They're in the Nether. We were able to defeat the army," said Nancy.

Brett couldn't believe they had destroyed the army. They were outnumbered. He didn't have time to ask them how they defeated Theo and his army, because his friends were pushing him onto the portal. It wasn't until they were in the Nether and the purple mist faded that Brett remembered his inventory was almost empty. He had given most of his items to the soldier. He was only left with his diamond sword, a potion of harming, and two snowballs. When three ghasts instantly attacked them, he didn't have a bow and arrow to fight back. He used his fists, but the flame from the fireball burned his hands, leaving him in pain.

"Are you okay?" asked Nancy.

"Where are your bow and arrow?" asked Poppy.

"The soldiers emptied most of my inventory. I hardly have anything. They were about to put me in prison," said Brett.

Poppy had a spare bow, but only a few arrows. "Take this." She handed him the bow and arrows.

A voice called out in the distance, "Guys! Over here!"

Eva stood next to Joe, Helen, and a group of people he didn't recognize. Brett sprinted toward them, and Eva introduced her friends. "These are the alchemists who were trapped in the Nether. Theo placed them all around the Nether, and most of them escaped and were reunited. We were lucky we found them. They were very helpful in slaying Theo and his army," explained Eva.

An alchemist with purple hair said, "We have to hide. Theo will be back. He will want revenge for our attack. I'm sure he's infuriated that we destroyed him and his army."

Another alchemist with flaming red hair in braids

added, "He's probably also very upset that we escaped. He wanted us to be trapped forever."

"We have to find the portal and go back in time," Eva announced, "and I think we found the Nether fortress where I was trapped. That is the one with the portal."

"Where is it?" asked Brett.

"This way," Eva called out as she sprinted through the fiery Nether, leading them up a large bridge and through an area with a lava river. Brett thought it looked familiar, and he hoped Eva was leading them to the right fortress.

"Here we are," Eva said as they approached the fortress. Again, the cluster of blazes that guarded the fortress met them. When the blazes saw the gang, they rose from the ground and initiated an attack.

The group collectively attacked the blazes, and Brett took the snowballs from his inventory and struck one of the fiery beasts. It was easier to defeat the blazes now that they had a large group. As they entered the fortress, Brett counted the alchemists. There were seven of them not including Eva.

"We found Eva right through here," said Poppy.

Brett's heart raced. He hoped this was the right fortress and they would find a hole in the wall.

"I see it!" exclaimed Poppy. "I see the hole!"

Poppy led them through the hole and headed to the door. She opened it, and a burst of cold air filled the room. "This is it! This is the portal!"

The gang walked into the hallway. Brett was freezing as he made the journey back in time. The trip felt like an eternity. He hoped when they reached the other side that they would be back in their old time period, but he wasn't certain this was the case. He had traveled through portals before and they landed him in all different time periods. The sweat on his blond hair turned to ice as he walked deeper into the portal. When they finally reached the other side, they were in a Nether fortress and were gloomily greeted by six wither skeletons.

The wither skeletons struck each of them as they emerged from the portal. Luckily, Brett had his diamond sword, and he struck one of them. The gang engaged in a battle against the wither skeletons. As Brett destroyed another wither skeleton, he wondered where they would emerge once they crafted a portal and left the Nether. He wondered if they would find Theo in this time period, and he hoped they could stop him before he destroyed the future.

When the final wither skeleton was destroyed, they sprinted out of the Nether fortress. Poppy ignited the portal back to the Overworld. Brett hoped they'd emerge in a time where Meadow Mews still existed.

11

BACK HOME

The purple mist lifted, and as they stepped off the portal, Poppy exclaimed, "It's your house, Brett!" Poppy rushed to Brett's house and opened the door; the others followed closely behind. She raced to the brewing stand filled with the empty bottles, remarking, "It's as if we never left."

Brett laughed as he looked at his small living room filled with eight alchemists from the future. "No, we definitely left."

The alchemists crowded around the brewing stand. One of the alchemists suggested they brew a bunch of potions so they could prepare for an attack against Theo. .

"Sounds like a plan," said Brett.

Joe added, "We have to find Theo. Do you have any idea where he is from? Where he lived before he destroyed the Overworld and took over Hillsdale?"

"No," said Eva, "but I think we should go to Hillsdale. Maybe he is from there and that's why he didn't destroy it."

Brett agreed that Hillsdale was a good place to start. "We have to come up with a plan. We can't just show up there."

Eva suggested, "We should make lots of bottles of the potion of invisibility. We can use that to explore the town and to see if we can spot Theo."

"Good idea," said the alchemist with the flaming red hair. "I also think we should note that Theo might not be dressed in his yellow robe. He might have had a different skin in the past."

Eva said, "It doesn't matter what he wears. I'll never forget his face. He has orange hair, and he always wears those dark sunglasses."

"I think we'll know who he is when we find him," said Brett.

Nancy and Helen suggested gathering fruits and other foods for the trip to Hillsdale and left the house.

The alchemists worked tirelessly to create the potions. They worked all day, and when night was setting in, Brett looked out his window and suggested that he craft beds for the eight alchemists.

"That would be great," said Eva, not looking up from the brewing stand. Brett marveled at how many bottles of potion were filled. They had brewed potions to heal, potions to harm, potions to make them faster, potions to help them see at night, and various other types of potions.

Brett, Poppy, and Joe crafted beds for them, then heard the sound of thunder.

"Aren't Nancy and Helen gathering fruit?" asked Joe.

"Yes," Brett replied.

"We have to help them. They can be attacked in the rain," said Joe.

Eva was holding a spider eye in one hand and bottle in the other. "Do you need our help?"

"You guys should stay here and keep brewing. Hopefully this storm won't last very long," said Brett.

As they raced out into the dark rainy night, Brett spotted two zombies with their arms extended. The vacant-eyed creatures lunged toward them, and Brett struck the smelly beasts with his diamond sword. After destroying both of the zombies with two strikes from his sword, he felt very confident, but everything changed when he saw a chicken jockey racing in his direction. The zombie riding the chicken ran into Brett, leaving him with one heart. Poppy raced to his side, striking the zombie with her sword and handing a potion of healing to Brett. He sipped the potion and destroyed the chicken.

"We can feast on this later," he said as he placed the soggy chicken into his inventory.

"Help!" Helen cried out in the distance.

"Where are you?" Poppy called out. "Helen, we can't find you." It was dark, and the rain made it harder to see. Brett, Poppy, and Joe searched for Helen as her cries grew fainter.

"We are going in the wrong direction," said Brett.

Nancy raced over toward them. She had one heart left, and she panted as she said, "They have Helen."

"Who?" questioned Brett.

"The soldiers," she replied.

"Where did they go?" asked Poppy.

"I don't know, but we have to find her," Nancy said.

Brett felt a pain in his shoulder, and he turned around to see three skeletons aiming their bows and arrows at the group. The rain was still falling, and he was exhausted. He didn't want to battle another mob, but he had no choice. He splashed a potion on the skeletons and was about to hit them with his diamond sword, but the rain stopped and they disappeared.

The gang sprinted back inside the house and screamed out in horror when they saw the alchemists surrounding Eva. Two of the alchemists were holding diamond swords against her unarmored chest.

"Help me!" Eva cried.

Brett looked at the alchemists, and he stared at Eva. He wondered if his first instinct was correct. Maybe she shouldn't have been trusted.

12

THE EIGHT ALCHEMISTS

"Help me!" Eva called out again.

"What is going on here?" Poppy pointed her diamond sword at the alchemists.

"Eva is a traitor. She works for Theo," one of the alchemists screamed.

"No, I don't," Eva screamed back. "I would never. I don't understand why you think that."

"You were the one who told Theo where we were," said the alchemist with flaming red hair. She was angry, and her face turned red. It almost matched her hair.

"I did," Eva confessed, "but it wasn't because I was on Theo's side. He told me that he put me on hardcore mode and that if I didn't tell him where we had been hiding, he would destroy me. He said that if I told him where you guys were, we would all be put in prison, but we'd survive. That is what happened: he imprisoned us

all, but we did survive. I knew that if we survived, one
day we'd be reunited and could defeat Theo."

"You ratted us out." The redheaded alchemist
struck Eva with her sword. Eva wailed in pain as she
lost a heart.

"Stop! I'm sorry," Eva cried.

"We spent decades in that prison." The alchemist
struck Eva again. "You're lucky that we were sly and
were able to hide things in our inventories so we could
eventually escape. If not, we would still be rotting away
in a Nether prison." The alchemist struck Eva another
time, and she was losing hearts.

"Stop!" Poppy screamed. "You don't have to
destroy Eva over this." Poppy handed Eva a potion of
strength. Poppy said, "We can't let what happened in
the past—"

Brett corrected her, "You mean the future."

"Whatever," Poppy said. "The point is, now we
are all working to destroy Theo. If we can destroy him
now, then Eva will never have to betray her allies."

"That's true," said the redheaded alchemist as she
put down her sword.

Eva said, "I am truly sorry. I was so worried that
I would be destroyed forever, and I knew I'd never be
able to help you. I thought Theo was going to put us
in prison together and we could fight him as a group.
I never thought he'd leave me trapped in a Nether fortress, where I was subjected to daily attacks from wither
skeletons, magma cubes, blazes, and all sorts of mobs
that live in that horrid biome. I never meant to betray

or hurt you guys. You are my best friends. We are the eight alchemists."

Nancy said, "I know you guys have issues from your past that you must resolve, but we have another problem to solve."

"Is it more important than this one?" asked an alchemist.

"Helen was taken by Theo's soldiers," Nancy said.

"Oh no!" the alchemists let out a collective cry.

Eva said, "We have to find her. We must save her and stop Theo."

"I know," said Nancy. "But how?"

"Let's go to Hillsdale," said Eva.

Brett reminded them that it was the middle of the night and any trip might be fatal. "We have to wait until morning. There's no point in depleting all of our energy battling hostile mobs."

The gang agreed, and Eva suggested they get some sleep. As they all crawled into their beds, Poppy asked, "How did you guys become the eight alchemists?"

"Before Theo launched his severe attack on the Overworld," said Eva, "we all lived together in Farmer's Bay. We had met while participating in a brewing contest, and we got along. We thought it would be great if we created a building, sort of like a lab and a factory, where we could brew and experiment and sell potions. People traveled from across the Overworld to trade with us and get our potions. Theo wasn't happy about this, because people weren't paying attention to the potions *he* brewed. He became very jealous, right, Sophie?"

The redheaded alchemist, Sophie, replied, "Yes, he started to terrorize us, and then while Eva was out gathering ingredients in the Nether, he captured us."

"That was when I was trapped in the fortress," said Eva. "I've never been back to our old place."

"It was destroyed." Sophie's eyes filled with tears. "He made us watch as he blew up our home with TNT."

The other alchemists began to cry and talk about intricate details they remembered from the factory. They all missed their old life very much, but Sophie said, "Once we saw you in the Nether, we were elated. We also saw that you had gathered a group of people to help you battle Theo. However, when we realized you were the one who betrayed us, we were heartbroken."

"Don't you understand what I was thinking? Can you ever forgive me?" Eva pleaded.

"Yes," said Sophie. "And I hope that we can defeat Theo and return to our home, even if we have to rebuild it."

"I'm so glad you still want me to be a part of the eight alchemists," said Eva.

Brett reminded them, "We should get some sleep. We have to battle Theo in the morning, and we need to be well rested."

Everyone agreed, but they had a hard time falling asleep. Nancy kept thinking about Helen being in the prison by herself. She imagined Helen being forced to give over all of her possessions before they forced her into the cold bedrock prison.

Brett also had trouble falling asleep. He was worried

about the battle. He also hoped they'd be able to save Meadow Mews. What if they weren't strong enough to overcome Theo and his army? As he tried to close his eyes and get some rest, he came up with a plan. He would tell all the residents of Meadow Mews, Verdant Valley, and all of the other neighboring towns about Theo. If everyone in the Overworld knew their future fate, they would all get together to stop him. Of course, he knew that some people might not believe him. Most people didn't think anyone could travel in time, so how could he explain that they traveled through an icy portal, in the Nether of all places, and wound up seeing a future where their towns were destroyed? These were the thoughts that raced through his head as he tried to close his eyes and drift off to sleep. When the sun shone through the window and woke Brett up in the morning, he was shocked that he had fallen asleep. He was even more shocked when he saw Helen standing in the doorway of his home. Her blue T-shirt was stained, and she brushed her long red hair from her face as she called out, "I escaped."

"Helen!" Nancy exclaimed.

"We have to get out of here," Helen warned them. "And we have to do it fast."

The eight alchemists ran to the brewing station and handed out bottles of potions to the group.

"Faster," Helen screamed. "They're coming!"

13
POP-UP PORTALS

Helen stood in the doorway. "I see them!"

Eva ordered everyone to splash a potion of invisibility on themselves and be still and quiet.

The gang listened to Eva, and soon they had all vanished. Three soldiers dressed in yellow appeared at the doorway. They looked through the house. One of the soldiers said, "It looks like they aren't here."

"But where could they have gone? We saw her racing this way."

Brett's heart beat quickly, and he hoped it wasn't beating so loudly that they could hear it. He also worried the potion would wear off, and that made his heart beat even faster. He wanted to take a deep breath, but he was worried they'd hear him. He stood as still and silent as he could while he listened to the soldiers.

"They must have bolted when they saw us," said

one of the soldiers as he exited. The other two followed closely behind.

The second they left the house, the potion wore off. Eva smiled. "Good timing, right?"

Brett said, "If the soldiers are already dressed in yellow, we can assume that Theo is wearing the skin with the yellow robe."

"We have to head to Hillsdale," said Poppy, her eyes filled with tears. "I am going to have to put TNT in my ice castle and blow it up. It's the only way we can weaken Theo."

"That seems rather drastic," said Sophie. "Perhaps we can try to battle another way."

"This is war," declared Poppy. "It *is* drastic."

"I know, but there might be other ways," said Nancy.

As they sprinted toward Hillsdale, they heard a loud roar. Poppy looked up and spotted an Ender Dragon flying in circles above them. She was shocked when she saw the eight alchemists take out bottles rather than their bows and arrows.

"What are you doing?" questioned Poppy.

"If you capture the purple clouds the Ender Dragon omits, you can create dragon's breath, which is a precious item when crafting certain rare potions," said Eva.

"Can you stop thinking like an alchemist and start thinking like an ally?" screamed Poppy.

Sophie asked, "Can't we do both?"

The dragon flew directly at them, and when purple clouds rushed toward them, Poppy used this opportunity to shoot a succession of arrows at the beast, as the eight alchemists fought one another for access to the cloud. Poppy never realized how competitive they seemed to be with one another. She watched as Brett bravely struck his diamond sword into the dragon's muscular side, but the dragon swung its wing at Brett, and he fell back.

Joe, Nancy, and Helen threw snowballs and shot arrows at the dragon, trying to destroy the beast, so they could end the battle and make their way to Hillsdale. The Ender Dragon was strong, and it wasn't easily defeated. It flew toward the group and roared. Poppy took a deep breath as the dragon flew inches from her, and she shot an arrow that landed on the dragon's face. The dragon was weakened and angry. It lunged at Poppy, but Brett slammed his diamond sword into its side, and the dragon started to lose hearts. It didn't have the energy to fight back and began emitting lights. The dragon faltered, and when it was destroyed, a portal to the End appeared in front of them.

The eight alchemists stood by the portal, but Poppy warned them, "Stay away. You don't want to go to the End."

"Why not?" asked Eva.

"We can't be distracted right now. We have to go to Hillsdale and battle Theo," she reminded them.

"He's obviously the one who spawned the Ender Dragon," added Joe.

"You're right," said Eva, and the alchemists walked away from the portal.

The gang was about to set off toward Hillsdale

when the skies turned dark and rain fell from the sky. A large army of zombies spawned in the town ready to attack them. The smell from the zombies was overpowering, and Brett felt sick. The alchemists splashed potions on the zombies as Poppy battled a skeleton.

Poppy was so distracted by the fight with the skeleton that she didn't realize the portal to the End was right behind her. She fell onto it and disappeared. Brett noticed Poppy fall into the End and screamed, "Poppy is in the End! We have to save her."

"I thought we had to go to Hillsdale," remarked Eva.

"Not now!" Brett screamed. "We have to help her before the portal disappears." As he sprinted to the portal, a skeleton shot an arrow that landed on his arm. He screamed out in pain and realized that he only had one heart left. He didn't battle the skeleton; instead, he grabbed a potion of healing and hopped onto the portal. He didn't look back to see who was following him into the End. He had to find Poppy and help her in this deathly world.

It seemed like the trip to the End took less than a second. Before he was able to readjust his armor, he was already standing on a platform in the End. He called out for Poppy, but there was no response.

14

THE END DOESN'T
MEAN IT'S OVER

"Poppy," Brett called out again.

"Over here!" she replied, and he followed the sound of her voice. When he saw her, she said, "Shh!" She pointed to the Ender Dragon. "We have to break the Ender crystals."

Brett shot an arrow at the Ender crystals, destroying one batch, which angered the Ender Dragon, who blew a fireball in their direction. They barely escaped being struck by the Ender Dragon. Brett shot an arrow at it while Poppy aimed to break the rest of the Ender crystals so the Ender Dragon couldn't replenish its energy.

Brett shot another arrow, but he was running low. Although his friends helped him replenish his inventory, they didn't have enough arrows to give him. He only had a couple of snowballs left and worried that he wouldn't be able to battle the Ender Dragon much longer. Poppy broke another group of Ender crystals, and she noticed Brett fumbling with a snowball.

"Are you okay?" she asked.

"I'm almost out of arrows," he replied. "I only have this snowball left. I can't fight the dragon."

Poppy grabbed a bunch of arrows from her inventory and handed them to Brett. As she gave him the arrows, the angry Ender Dragon shot a fireball at them, and they were almost hit.

"Remember when our biggest problem was figuring out which prank we were going to play on our friends?" Poppy missed the leisurely days she spent with Brett. When their life was peaceful, they were always planning funny pranks and hanging out. When they worked, they built challenging structures and farms and enjoyed their jobs. However, when people attacked them, they were forced into a world that was challenging and not fun at all. Maybe some people found battling fun, but that wasn't the way they found happiness.

Brett used one of Poppy's arrows to strike the Ender Dragon as it flew toward the last batch of Ender crystals. As Poppy hit and broke the crystals, Brett's arrow pierced the dragon's flesh. He shot another arrow, then heard people in the distance.

"We're not alone," he called out.

"We can't pay attention to anybody else. The Ender crystals are gone. This is our opportunity to destroy the dragon fast," she said as she shot an arrow at the Ender Dragon. It wasn't hit and flew away.

Brett was distracted by the sound of people as he aimed his arrow at the dragon. He had one eye on the distance, looking out for an attack from Theo or whoever might be in the End. He feared Theo would try to trap them in the End.

Poppy shot another arrow at the Ender Dragon and destroyed it. She was thrilled, and Brett commended her, "Great job, but we have to get out of here now."

A group of Endermen walked toward them. The duo tried not to lock eyes with them, as the voices in the distance grew louder. Brett turned around and smiled when he saw Joe, Helen, Nancy, and the alchemists.

"You destroyed the Ender Dragon!" Joe called out.

"Poppy did it!" exclaimed Brett.

"I see the End city," said Helen. "Should we go there?"

"No," Brett reminded her. "Now that the Ender Dragon is gone, we can return to the Overworld."

"But we just got here," said Helen.

"And you're lucky you get to leave this quickly. The End isn't fun at all," said Brett.

The gang went through a portal and emerged in the Overworld. As they spawned in Meadow Mews, they were caught in a storm and were standing face-to-face with Theo and his army.

"We are in my time period," Brett said as he swung his sword at Theo, "and there's no way I am going to let you destroy the towns that I love."

Theo laughed as he splashed a potion on Brett. Brett was so wet from the rain that he couldn't even feel the potion on his body, but he felt the effects. His body slowed down, he felt very tired, and he could barely move.

Poppy leaped at Theo, and Eva handed Brett a potion of recovery. The rain was falling harder, but there were only a couple of hostile mobs in the town. The alchemists battled the hostile mobs while Poppy and Brett focused on destroying Theo.

"What is wrong with you, Theo?" asked Brett. "Why are you trying to ruin the Overworld?"

"Ruin it?" Theo asked. "I am making it better. I am transforming it into the perfect world for me."

"For you?" Poppy slammed her diamond sword into Theo's unarmored shoulder. "You aren't the only person in the Overworld, if you haven't noticed. Why don't you think about other people? If you did, you'd see they aren't very happy with the way you are acting."

"I have a group of soldiers who are very happy," he said as he pierced Poppy's leg with his diamond sword.

"Are you guys happy?" Poppy asked as the soldiers attacked Nancy, Helen, and Joe. They didn't respond; they just lashed out at the group with their swords.

"They aren't going to respond to you. You are a prisoner, and what you say doesn't matter," said Theo as he struck Poppy again, leaving her with one heart.

The rain stopped, and the alchemists joined them in the battle against Theo. Poppy thought they had a solid advantage now that they had an additional eight people who came with an arsenal of potions. However, her outlook changed when she saw a group of soldiers march into Meadow Mews. She tried to count them as they stormed into town, but there were so many that she lost count. Counting the soldiers distracted her, and Theo used this opportunity to deliver a final blow that destroyed Poppy.

She awoke in Brett's house and looked out the window to see what was happening with Theo's soldiers and her friends, but when she looked out the window, she didn't see anybody there. This shocked Poppy, and she wondered how they disappeared so quickly. She ran out of the house and sprinted into the streets of Meadow Mews looking for Brett and her friends, but it was eerily empty. She looked for any neighbors that she knew, but nobody was home. Poppy made her way to Hillsdale on her own. She hoped that once she arrived in Hillsdale, she would be reunited with her friends. Or hopefully, she'd see them on the way. As she hurried through the Overworld, the temperature began to drop, and her teeth chattered. She walked through the snow and turned around when she heard a voice call out.

"Poppy! Stop!"

15

BLIZZARD

"**P**oppy." Eva dashed over to her. "It's a trap."

"What?" asked Poppy, but Eva didn't have time to explain. The soldiers surrounded her and demanded that she had to empty her inventory.

"No," she screamed and leaped at one of the soldiers with her diamond sword, but they splashed a potion on her, and she was weakened. Her arms couldn't move, and she dropped the diamond sword on the ground.

"Good job," said the soldier with a smirk as he picked up the diamond sword. "Now you have to give us the rest of your items."

From the corner of her eye, Poppy could see Eva standing next to a soldier who emptied her inventory. The soldier marveled at the various potions in her inventory. "Wow," he said. "What a find. I won't have to brew for a very long time."

The soldier emptying Poppy's inventory reminded

him that all potions and finds from prisoners' inventories must be handed over to Theo. "Oh, right," said the soldier as he walked Eva over to Poppy. "Now we have to bring them to the prison with the others."

Poppy was upset that she would be in the bedrock prison, but she was glad to be reunited with her friends. She knew once she was reunited with them, they would be able to come up with a plan to escape. They would fight back, even if they didn't have weapons. They were creative and were in situations like this before and made it out—although they had never been stripped of all their possessions. She walked alongside Eva as they were marched inside the prison.

"Poppy," Brett said as he stood by the gates. "They got you."

"I hope you weren't thinking I'd get you guys out of here." Tears filled her eyes as she spoke.

"No, I'm just glad you're okay," he said and walked to the small window in the corner of the prison cell and looked out.

Poppy walked over to the window and looked out. "It looks like the snow is blowing around. I think a storm is coming."

Eva and the alchemists clustered together, talking in hushed voices. Nancy, Helen, and Joe approached them, and Nancy asked, "Are you guys coming up with a plan?"

Eva spoke in a raised whisper, "Sophie never emptied her inventory. The soldier forgot to do it. She has a bunch of potions. If we distribute them, we can use them to attack the soldier who comes to feed us, and we can escape."

Poppy and Brett were standing by the window and didn't hear the plan. They were watching the beginnings of a blizzard. Snow flew past them as the winds continued to pick up. A gust of wind blew two soldiers across Hillsdale. Poppy tried not to laugh. Snow began to fall, and skeletons spawned outside the window. Poppy liked watching the soldiers battle the skeletons. They were having a hard time battling the mobs in the windy weather. She finally let out a chuckle when she saw a soldier's diamond sword blow away as he attempted to lunge at a skeleton.

"What's so funny?" asked Eva as she handed Poppy a bottle of potion.

"Where did you get this?" asked Poppy.

"Didn't you hear? Sophie has a fully stocked inventory. We are going to use these potions to escape when the soldier comes to feed us."

Eva handed Brett potions. He thanked her and said, "But even if we escape, how are we going to survive a battle in this blizzard?"

Eva stared out the window. "Wow, that's an intense storm. I've never witnessed anything like that before."

The wind created snowdrifts that buried the soldiers, and zombies and skeletons left footprints in the heavy snow. The gang crowded around the window to watch this epic blizzard when the soldier came with their daily meal.

"We have to do it now," said Eva. Poppy wasn't

convinced this was the best timing, but there was no time to debate because Eva splashed a potion on the soldier, the other alchemists joined in, and he was destroyed. They grabbed the plate of apples and devoured them, leaving some for Poppy and the others. As the alchemists sprinted out of the prison cell, they clutched potions and attacked every soldier they encountered.

Brett and Poppy followed them out. Brett remarked, "It's so cold. It's colder than walking through or falling down a portal."

"I know." Poppy shivered. "This is unbearable."

Two zombies leaped at the duo, and they splashed potions on them. Brett said, "This is going to be an awful battle unless we get our supplies back."

Poppy said, "I have a plan," and she hurried toward a soldier battling a skeleton. She held a potion next to his face. "Give me a diamond sword now!" she demanded.

The soldier had one heart left, and the skeleton was about to shoot an arrow at him. The soldier didn't reply, and Poppy was infuriated and grabbed his sword from his hand as the skeleton shot an arrow that ripped into the soldier's shoulder, destroying him.

"We need to get weapons from the soldiers," she said to Brett as she struck the skeleton with the soldier's diamond sword, obliterating him. Then she picked up the bone it dropped on the snowy ground.

The snow was falling harder, and the snowdrifts were getting deeper. As they approached another soldier, ready to empty him of his inventory, Theo slammed his diamond sword into Brett's back, shouting, "What do you think you're doing?"

16

THE JOURNEY

"Stop this nonsense!" Brett said as he splashed a potion on Theo. Poppy plunged her diamond sword into Theo's arm. He had one heart left.

"Help! Army!" Theo could barely get out the words.

Only two soldiers could hear him through the noisy wind, but they were struggling to battle a gang of skeletons.

Poppy pressed her sword against Theo's yellow robe. "One more strike from this sword, and you're destroyed."

"So, I'll just respawn in my ice castle." He smiled.

"My ice castle," Poppy corrected him. "And you won't respawn there. I have command blocks, and I have placed everyone on hardcore mode."

"You didn't do that," said Theo.

"Poppy doesn't lie," said Brett.

"If you don't believe me," she said as she pressed her

sword a little deeper, "I can destroy you, and you'll find out if I am lying."

"No," Theo said. "Don't."

Poppy led Theo toward the cold, damp bedrock prison and marched him into the cell. "Look." She pointed to an apple on the ground. "There's your dinner."

"If I stay in here, will you take me off hardcore mode?" asked Theo.

"Maybe," Poppy said as she locked the gate. "But you were never on hardcore mode."

Theo looked at Brett. "I thought you said Poppy never lies."

Brett smiled. "I never said *I* didn't."

Poppy and Brett sprinted from the cold prison, and Poppy called out, "Theo is captured. Everyone must surrender."

Surprisingly, the snow stopped and the soldiers walked toward them. One soldier cheered, and the others joined him.

"Theo is really in prison?" questioned a soldier in disbelief.

"Yes," said Poppy. "And we will keep a close eye on him because we don't want him destroying the Overworld."

One of the soldiers asked, "Was that his plan? He never said that."

"We've seen the future," Poppy said, "and he was going to destroy most of the towns and force people to become soldiers and live in the ice castle. Luckily, this was just the beginning, and we were able to stop him before he destroyed our towns."

One soldier called out, "Liar! Theo was trying to make this a better world. He was leading us."

"How can you make a place better by ruining it and capturing the people who live there? That doesn't make sense," said Brett.

As they spoke to the soldier, Eva and the alchemists came over along with Joe, Nancy, and Helen. Eva asked, "What happened?"

"We've captured Theo," declared Brett.

"That means I can go home, right?" asked Eva.

Brett and Poppy hoped they'd be able to help Eva and the alchemists return back to their time period, but they knew that the portals weren't very reliable. You never knew when and if you'd find one, and if you did, where you'd wind up. Poppy said, "We will try to get you back home."

"We should try to craft a portal to the Nether," said Sophie.

"Yes," said Poppy. "But first I want to make sure Theo will be watched and that the army will happily change back to their old skins."

Before she even finished her sentence, a group of soldiers changed back into their old skins, but there were two soldiers who remained dressed in yellow. The two soldiers in yellow raced toward Poppy and Brett with their diamond swords and struck them.

"We are going to release Theo from prison," one of them screamed as he bolted toward the bedrock prison.

Eva and the alchemists rushed after the soldier. "Give up," Eva ordered. "Your leader isn't going to destroy the Overworld, and neither are you two."

Eva splashed a potion on the soldiers, leaving them weakened and with one heart each. The alchemists escorted the two soldiers into the prison.

"You have company," Eva said as she placed the two soldiers into the prison cell.

As she walked toward the gate to close it, Theo splashed a potion on her. "You never emptied our inventories." Theo laughed as a soldier swung his diamond sword at Eva, destroying her. The three prisoners escaped, tearing out of the bedrock prison.

"They've escaped!" hollered Brett and Poppy in unison.

Theo was about to splash a potion of invisibility when Sophie knocked the bottle from his hand.

"You aren't going to be invisible. You're going back to prison," she said as she splashed a potion on Theo, but the soldiers attacked Sophie.

Poppy, Brett, and Joe raced over to help Sophie, but they were too late. She was destroyed. Poppy screamed at Theo, "Just surrender. It's pointless. You lost."

"Never!" Theo said. "I will win!"

Six of Theo's former soldiers ran over to him. One of them said, "We used to be your soldiers. You probably don't recognize us because we are dressed in clothes that we chose for ourselves. You better give up because, even if you escape, we will spend our lives finding you and making sure you never attack another town again."

Another soldier said, "We know that you were going destroy towns across the Overworld."

"I know, I had such a promising future," remarked Theo.

17

NETHER FOREVER

Poppy thought she could see tears in Theo's eyes when she walked him back to the bedrock prison alongside his former soldiers. Theo and his last two remaining soldiers stood silently as Poppy locked the gate.

She was about to leave when she pulled out a large chest. "Please empty your inventories. I want to place all of your items in here. Once we feel that you aren't going to threaten the Overworld, we will release you and let you have everything back."

The trio reluctantly emptied their inventories. Theo questioned, "You're really going to give our stuff back?"

"Yes," said Poppy, "when we know you aren't interested in hurting others anymore. See, when you took people's inventories, it was for your benefit, and you never planned on returning it. You simply stole it."

"There is nothing simple about that," said Brett.

One of the soldiers asked, "Can I change my skin before we give up all of our items? I don't want to be part of Theo's army anymore."

"Me neither," said the other soldier.

Eva and Sophie had returned to Hillsdale and rushed into the bedrock prison. "There's a storm!"

A thunderous boom was heard outside.

Theo said, "The storm is my fault."

"What?" ask Brett.

"I have command blocks in a cave outside of town, and I am manipulating the weather."

"We have to break those command blocks," said Brett.

Joe and Brett hurried out to find the command blocks and to break them into pieces, so the storms would stop.

The wind rattled the small window in the cell, and a skeleton spawned inside the prison.

Eva struck the skeleton as Poppy continued to take items from Theo's inventory.

"I hope Brett and Joe can stop the storm before it gets too intense," said Poppy.

Theo didn't say anything. He silently emptied his inventory and handed it to Poppy, who placed it in the chest.

As she placed Theo's and the soldiers' final item in the chest and closed it, Poppy was happy that the battle was over and the Overworld was saved, but she knew that they had to return to the Nether to help Eva and the alchemists. Despite everything, Poppy still disliked the Nether. She also liked Eva and was sad to see her go back to her time period.

There wasn't time to be sentimental, because four more skeletons spawned in the prison, and Poppy, Eva, Sophie, Nancy, Helen, and the alchemists began to battle bony beasts. Zombies were ripping the hinges from the prison's door when the snowstorm stopped.

"Do you think that happened on its own or because they destroyed the command blocks?" Poppy questioned.

"They destroyed it, I'm sure of it," said Theo.

Brett and Joe sprinted through the doorway to the prison. "The command blocks have been broken."

"Hallelujah," said Poppy.

"Now we get to go home," exclaimed Eva, and the alchemists cheered.

"Does anybody have obsidian?" asked Nancy.

Poppy looked through her inventory. "I've used all of mine because I crafted so many portals."

There was a period of silence as everyone checked if they had obsidian, and finally one of the former soldiers called out that he had some obsidian and offered it to the gang.

"Thanks." Poppy took the obsidian and placed it on the ground and began to craft a portal. "I hope we can all fit," she said as she looked at the eight alchemists and her friends.

"I think I should stay behind," said Nancy. "I want to make sure Theo stays in jail."

"I'll stay with you," said Helen.

Joe said, "I have to go to Verdant Valley to work on the farm, so I can't go."

Brett said, "When we get back, I will meet you in Verdant Valley."

Poppy hoped Brett was right and they would get back from the Nether. She was very nervous about this trip, and she understood why so many of her friends weren't going to be able to go with them, but she was secretly envious of them. She still disliked the Nether, but she knew that she couldn't complain. She had to help Eva and the alchemists make their way back home.

Poppy ignited the portal that sat on the snowy ground. As they were surrounded by purple mist, Poppy was happy that she was escaping the cold. She wasn't dressed for Hillsdale weather, and now she would warm up quickly. The trip to the Nether was fast, and within a second, they were surrounded in a world filled with lava waterfalls, zombie pigmen, and blazes.

"Ghasts!" Brett called out.

The gang aimed their bows and arrows and attacked these fiery mobs. Poppy shot an arrow at the final ghast, and a ghast tear fell to the netherrack ground. She handed the tear to Eva. "When you make a potion, I hope you will think of me."

Eva smiled. "I will think of you guys often. You've been so good to me. Sometimes I can't believe our luck."

Sophie said, "I can't believe that when we walk through this portal, we will be living in a peaceful world."

"We will be back in the lab and warehouse crafting all sorts of potions," said Eva.

The other alchemists reminded them that they had bottled the dragon's breath, and they were all teeming with excitement.

Poppy didn't want to ruin their happiness, but she did have to point out that she didn't see a Nether fortress.

Brett added, "You're right. Does anybody know which direction we should go?"

"I don't know." Eva was panicked. Just a few seconds before she had been excited about the return home, but now she wondered if they'd ever find the portal and feared they'd be stuck in the Nether forever.

"We will get you home. We will find the Nether fortress," Poppy promised them, but she wasn't sure she'd be able to keep the promise.

A group of four zombie pigmen walked past them. One of the alchemists walked too close to the zombie pigmen, and they began to attack the alchemist with their swords.

18

BREWING

The zombie pigmen were vicious and attacked the alchemists. Poppy and Brett struck the zombie pigmen with their diamond swords, and the alchemists splashed potions. When the final zombie pigman was destroyed, they picked up the gold nuggets the pigmen had dropped on the ground.

Eva called out, "Is that the fortress?"

Poppy looked off in the distance. She didn't see the fortress, but she followed Eva. She hoped it would come into view, but it felt as if they were walking forever, and they hadn't reached it. Poppy's forehead was covered in sweat, and she wanted to make a portal back to the Overworld when she saw the fortress ahead.

Eva and the alchemists charged the fortress and annihilated the blazes that stood guard before Poppy and Brett arrived. When they reached the fortress, they sprinted out and into the room with the hole. They crawled through the hole, but the room that housed the door to the portal was closed, and their alchemist friends were gone.

"They left without saying goodbye." Poppy looked at the ground, and her eyes filled with tears.

"They were excited, and sometimes goodbyes are easier short," Brett rationalized.

"That wasn't a short goodbye; it was a nonexistent one," said Poppy as she climbed through the hole. She heard a familiar voice.

"Poppy!" Eva called out.

Sophie said, "We just got the treasure from the fortress, so we have some loot to trade when we get back home."

"I thought you guys left without saying goodbye," said Poppy.

"We'd never do something like that," said Eva.

Sophie said, "I want to thank you guys. You've really helped us a lot."

Poppy said, "You're welcome, and I wish I could visit you."

"I know, it's so hard to say goodbye when we know we can't visit," said Poppy.

"I'm glad we met," said Eva as she approached the door.

"Poppy, we shouldn't be in here when the door opens to the portal," warned Brett. "We don't want to wind up in the future."

"Wait!" Poppy said to Eva before she opened the door. "Since we stopped Theo, that means that Meadow

Mews still exists. Can you visit us there? You can introduce yourself to my future self, and we can be friends."

"Of course," said Eva. "We'll all take a trip to Meadow Mews and find you guys."

"Now I have something to look forward to," said Poppy.

"Me too," said Eva.

Poppy and Brett exited the Nether fortress before they opened the door. They ran out of the fortress and created a portal back to the Overworld. When they emerged, they were in front of Brett's house.

Brett said, "I have to head to Verdant Valley to help Joe on his farm."

"Good luck," said Poppy. "I want to go home and brew potions with all of the ingredients from the Nether."

"Poppy! Brett!" Nancy and Helen called out as they raced over to them. "Did they find their way back in time?"

"Hopefully," said Poppy. "We did find the Nether fortress, and they entered the portal. We hope that it lands them in the right time period."

Brett looked up at the sky. "I have to excuse myself. It will be dark soon, and I'm going to travel to Verdant Valley to help Joe with the farm."

Nancy said, "It's going to be nice to be able to work on the farm without the fear of a rainstorm."

"I know," said Brett. "I am so glad we were able to destroy those command blocks."

Brett said goodbye and entered his house. Everything was back to normal, and his inventory still had a bunch of potions that the alchemists had brewed. He looked down at all of the beds on his floor. They covered almost every inch of his house. He was excited to work on the farm, but he was also sad that the adventure was over.

Outside he could hear Nancy, Helen, and Poppy going through their inventories. They were listing their remaining potions and the ones that they were going to brew. He also wished he could stay at home and brew with his friends or brainstorm ideas for new pranks with Poppy, but he packed up all of his farming equipment and a bunch of new seeds and started out on his journey to Verdant Valley.

The sun was about to set when he arrived in Verdant Valley. Joe was excited to see him and dashed over to Brett to greet him. Brett told Joe about the trip to the Nether and about saying goodbye to the alchemists.

"I guess I will meet them soon enough in Farmer's Bay, since that is where Eva is from," said Joe.

"They also promised to find us in Meadow Mews. It's strange to think that the alchemists might be hanging out with our future selves at this very moment," said Brett.

"I don't think it's strange; I think it's incredible," Joe said as he placed an irrigation system. Brett began to help him.

Brett began to dig a hole to create a second irrigation system. As he dug deep into the soil, he felt a rush of cold air and jumped back.

"Is everything okay?" asked Joe.

"I hope so," he replied. "I felt a burst of cold air when I was digging, and I was afraid it was another portal."

Joe looked down at the hole Brett had dug and said, "Let's just leave that area alone. I'm not ready to travel back or forward in time at the moment."

Joe placed a layer of dirt over the hole and dug another one far away from it. He placed the irrigation system, and was ready to put the seeds down. The sun was setting, and they had to finish up their work for the day. As they looked at the setting sun, they both smiled.

"It's good to have everything back to normal," said Joe.

"I agree," said Brett.

The duo walked back to the house Joe was staying at in Verdant Valley, chatting about the work they would do the following day.

"I think we should put potatoes down," said Brett.

"I think we should place lots of wheat," said Joe.

As they planned their farm, the sun set on another day in the Overworld.

The End